Thomas Hughes Children's Library
Chicago Public Library
400 South State Street
Chicago, IL 60605

PowerKids Readers:
The Bilingual Library of the United States of America™

*Bilingual Edition
English/Spanish
Edición bilingüe*

UTAH

JOSÉ MARÍA OBREGÓN
TRADUCCIÓN AL ESPAÑOL: MARÍA CRISTINA BRUSCA

The Rosen Publishing Group's
PowerKids Press™ & **Editorial Buenas Letras**™
New York

Published in 2006 by The Rosen Publishing Group, Inc.
29 East 21st Street, New York, NY 10010

Copyright © 2006 by The Rosen Publishing Group, Inc.

All rights reserved. No part of this book may be reproduced in any form without permission in writing from the publisher, except by a reviewer.

First Edition

Photo Credits: Cover © Scott T. Smith/Corbis; p. 5 © Joe Sohm/The Image Works; p. 7 © 2002 Geoatlas; p. 9 © Kent Meireis/The Image Works; p. 11 © George H. H. Huey/Corbis; pp. 13, 23, 31 (Flatland, Warrior) © Corbis; pp. 15, 31 (Smoot) © Bettmann/Corbis; p. 17 © Patrik Giardino/Corbis; pp. 19, 31 (S. Young) © Reuters/Corbis; p. 21 © Warren Morgan/Corbis; pp. 25, 30 (Capital) © David Ball/Corbis; p. 30 (Sego Lily) © Pat O'Hara/Corbis; p. 30 (California Gull) © Kevin Schafer/Corbis; pp. 30 (The Beehive State), 31 (Beehive) © Joe McDonald/Corbis; p. 30 (Blue Spruce) © Wolfgang Kaehler/Corbis; p. 31 (Cassidy) © Jonathan Blair/Corbis; p. 31 (Sorensen) Used by permission, Utah State Historical Society, all rights reserved; p. 31 (L. Young) © CinemaPhoto/Corbis; p. 31 (Woods) © Henry Diltz/Corbis

Library of Congress Cataloging-in-Publication Data

Obregón, José María, 1963–
  Utah / José María Obregón ; traducción al español, María Cristina Brusca.—1st ed.
       p. cm. — (The bilingual library of the United States of America)
  Includes bibliographical references and index.
  ISBN 1-4042-3110-2 (library binding)
  1. Utah–Juvenile literature. I. Title. II. Series.
  F826.3.O2718 2006
  979.2—dc22
                                                      2005028579

Manufactured in the United States of America

Due to the changing nature of Internet links, Editorial Buenas Letras has developed an online list of Web sites related to the subject of this book. This site is updated regularly. Please use this link to access the list:

http://www.buenasletraslinks.com/ls/utah

Contents

1. Welcome to Utah ... 4
2. Utah Geography ... 6
3. Utah History ... 12
4. Living in Utah ... 16
5. Utah Today ... 22
6. Let´s Draw the Map of Utah ... 26
   Timeline/Utah Events ... 28–29
   Utah Facts ... 30
   Famous Utahans/Words to Know ... 31
   Resources/Word Count/Index ... 32

Contenido

1. Bienvenidos a Utah ... 4
2. Geografía de Utah ... 6
3. Historia de Utah ... 12
4. La vida en Utah ... 16
5. Utah, hoy ... 22
6. Dibujemos el mapa de Utah ... 26
   Cronología/ Eventos en Utah ... 28–29
   Datos sobre Utah ... 30
   Utaheños famosos/ Palabras que debes saber ... 31
   Recursos/ Número de palabras/ Índice ... 32

Welcome to Utah

Utah is known as the Beehive State. In the center of the state seal you can see a beehive. This stands for the hard work of the people of Utah.

Bienvenidos a Utah

Utah es conocido como el Estado Colmena. En el centro del escudo del estado puedes ver una colmena. La colmena representa el trabajo arduo de los pobladores de Utah.

Utah Flag and State Seal

Bandera y escudo de Utah

Utah Geography

Utah borders the states of Arizona, Colorado, Idaho, Nevada, New Mexico, and Wyoming. Utah lies in the Rocky Mountain area of the United States.

Geografía de Utah

Utah linda con los estados de Arizona, Colorado, Idaho, Nevada, Nuevo México y Wyoming. Utah se encuentra en la región de las Montañas Rocosas.

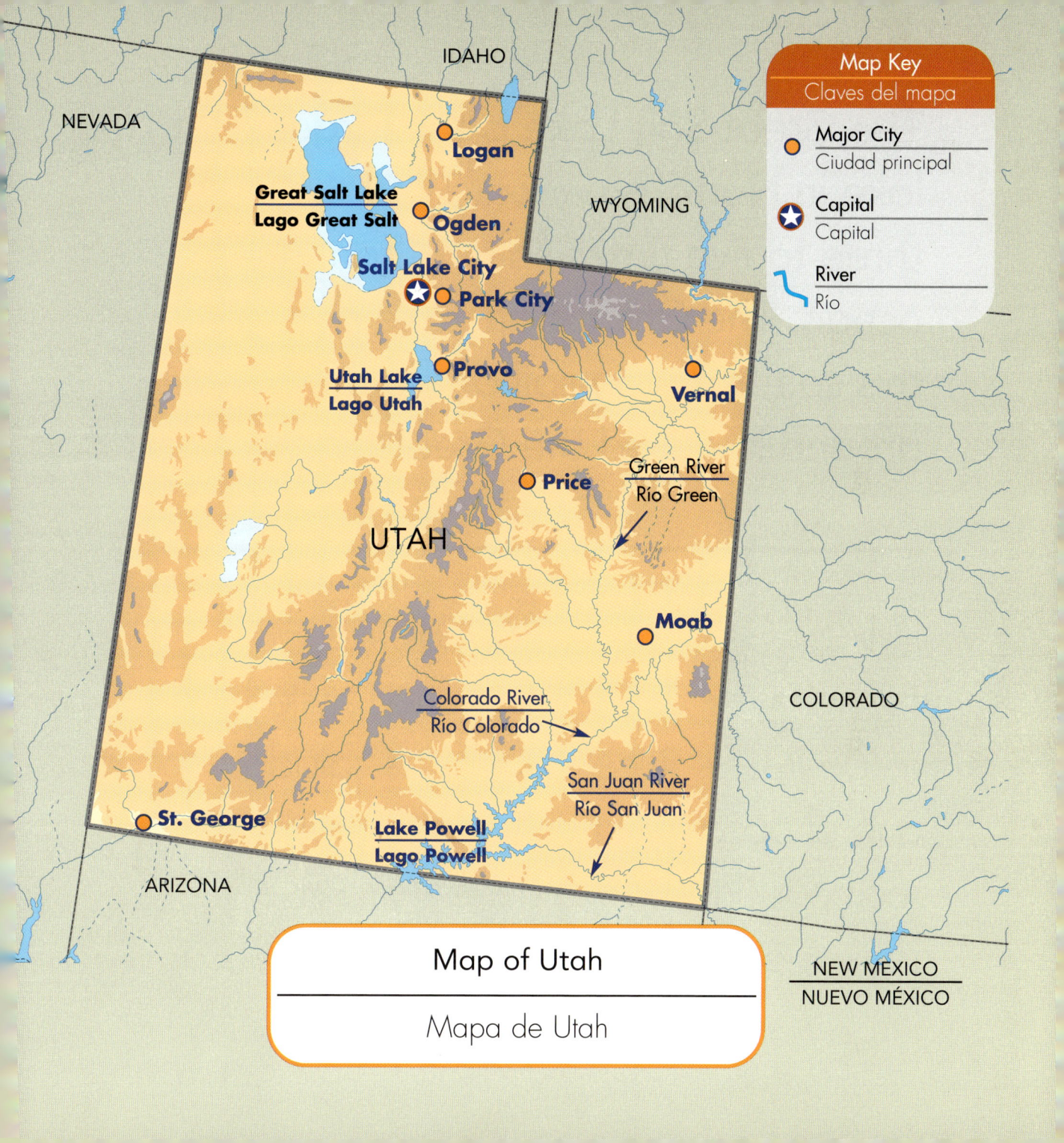

Map of Utah
Mapa de Utah

Map Key / Claves del mapa
- Major City / Ciudad principal
- Capital / Capital
- River / Río

Locations shown:
- Logan
- Ogden
- Salt Lake City (Capital)
- Park City
- Provo
- Vernal
- Price
- Moab
- St. George

Water features:
- Great Salt Lake / Lago Great Salt
- Utah Lake / Lago Utah
- Green River / Río Green
- Colorado River / Río Colorado
- San Juan River / Río San Juan
- Lake Powell / Lago Powell

Bordering states: IDAHO, WYOMING, COLORADO, NEW MEXICO / NUEVO MÉXICO, ARIZONA, NEVADA

The Great Salt Lake is the largest salt lake in North America. The lake is three to five times saltier than the ocean. The Great Salt Lake gets all this salt from the soil of the land area around it, called the Great Basin.

El lago Great Salt es el lago salado más grande de Norteamérica. Este lago es de tres a cinco veces más salado que el océano. El lago Great Salt recibe toda esta sal de la tierra que lo rodea, conocida como la Gran Cuenca.

The Great Salt Lake

Lago Great Salt

Utah is home to many natural wonders. The state has five national parks and six national forests. The Arches National Park in Utah has more than 2,000 natural stone arches.

En Utah se encuentran muchas maravillas de la naturaleza. El estado tiene cinco parques nacionales y seis bosques nacionales. En el Parque Nacional Los Arcos hay más de 2,000 arcos naturales de piedra.

Stone Arch at the Arches National Park

Un arco de piedra en el Parque Nacional Los Arcos

Utah History

Utah takes its name from a group of Native Americans called the Utes. The Utes and other groups, like the Shoshone and Paiute, have lived in Utah for thousands of years.

Historia de Utah

Utah tomó su nombre del grupo indígena americano llamado Ute. Los Ute y otros grupos nativoamericanos como los Shoshone y Paiute han vivido en Utah por miles de años.

Uinta Ute Warrior in 1874

Un guerrero Uinta Ute en 1874

Living in Utah

Utah is home to people of many different origins. Almost 200,000 Hispanics live in Utah. Hispanics are people who come from Spanish-speaking countries.

La vida en Utah

Utah es el hogar de muchas personas de diferentes orígenes. Casi 200,000 hispanos viven en Utah. Los hispanos son personas que vienen de países donde se habla el español.

Hispanic Kids on a Baseball Team

Niños hispanos en un equipo de béisbol

Every January since 1988, Park City, Utah has held the Sundance Film Festival. Many people visit the city then to watch movies and meet actors and film directors.

Cada enero, desde 1988, el Festival de cine Sundance ha tenido lugar en Park City, Utah. Muchas personas visitan la ciudad para ver las películas y conocer a los actores y directores de cine.

The Egyptian Theater in Park City, Utah

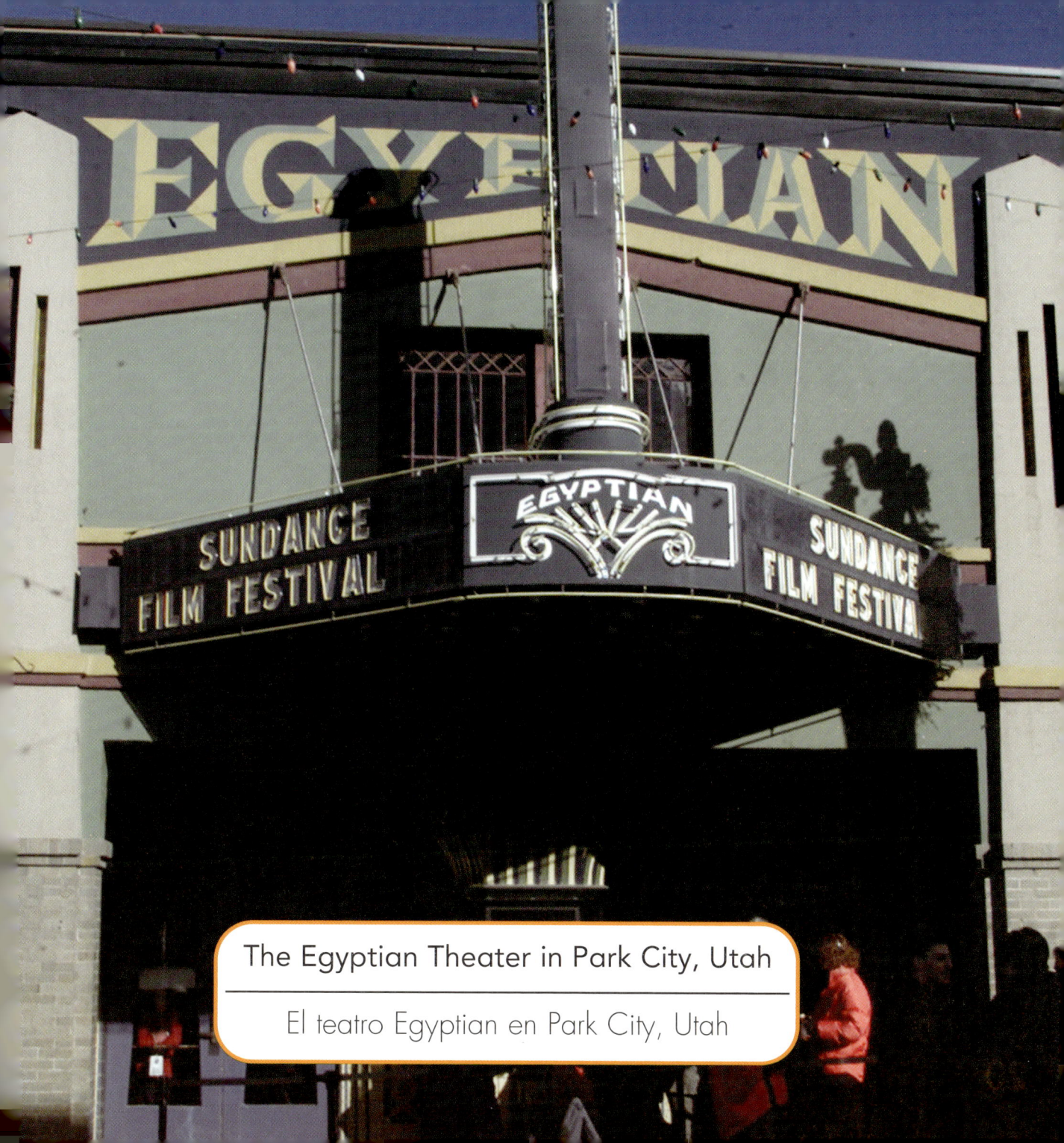

El teatro Egyptian en Park City, Utah

Many Utahans enjoy outdoor sports. The mountains in Utah are great places for outdoor sports like mountain biking and skiing. Alta, Park City, and Brian Head are famous places to ski.

Muchos utaheños disfrutan de los deportes al aire libre. Las montañas de Utah son lugares ideales para la práctica de deportes como el esquí y el *mountain biking*. Alta, Park City y Brian Head son famosos centros de esquí.

Skiers in Utah

Esquiadores en Utah

Utah Today

Arms and rockets have been tested by the army in the flatlands of Utah. Today many Utahans are working to stop this. Utahans are worried about the effect of these tests on the land.

Utah, hoy

En las llanuras de Utah se han probado armas de fuego y cohetes. Muchos utaheños trabajan para terminar con estas pruebas. Se preocupan por el efecto que podrían tener sobre su medio ambiente.

Missile Test in Western Utah

Prueba de un misil en el oeste de Utah

Salt Lake City, West Valley City, Provo, St. George, and Sandy are important cities in Utah. Salt Lake City is the capital of the state.

Salt Lake City, West Valley City, Provo, St. George y Sandy son ciudades importantes de Utah. Salt Lake City es la capital del estado.

Capitol Building in Salt Lake City, Utah

Capitolio en Salt Lake City, Utah

Activity:
Let´s Draw the Map of Utah

Actividad:
Dibujemos el mapa de Utah

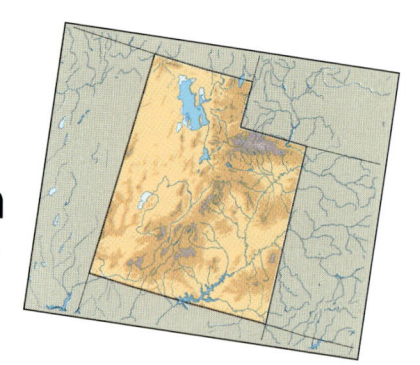

1 To begin draw a rectangle.

Para comenzar dibuja un rectángulo.

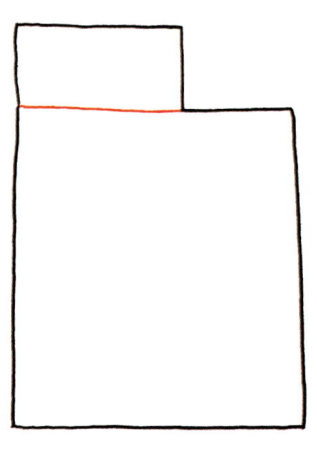

2 Draw a smaller rectangle on top of the first rectangle.

Dibuja un rectángulo más pequeño encima del primer rectángulo.

3

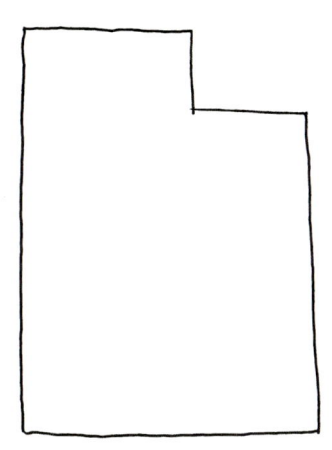

Erase the extra line.

Borra la línea sobrante.

4

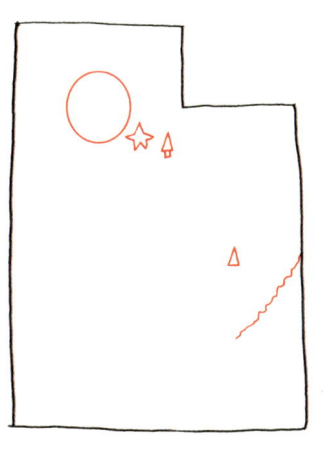

Now add some of Utah's special places to your map. Draw a triangle for the Arches National Park. Draw a squiggly line for the Colorado River. Draw a circle for the Great Salt Lake. Draw a star for Salt Lake City. Draw a tree shape for Park City.

Ahora, agrega a tu mapa algunos de los lugares importantes de Utah. Dibuja un triángulo en el lugar del Parque Nacional Los Arcos. Dibuja una línea ondulada para indicar el río Colorado. Traza un círculo en el sitio del lago Great Salt. Dibuja una estrella en el lugar de Salt Lake City. Traza una forma de árbol para indicar Park City.

Timeline | Cronología

Fathers Silvestre Vélez de Escalante and Francisco Atanasio Domínguez seek a new way from New Mexico to California and explore Utah.	**1776**	Los padres Silvestre Vélez de Escalante y Francisco Atanasio Domínguez buscan una nueva ruta de Nuevo México a California y exploran Utah.
Mexico wins independence from Spain and claims Utah.	**1821**	México declara su independencia de España y reclama Utah.
The first group of Mormons arrive in the Salt Lake Valley to build a new home.	**1847**	El primer grupo de pioneros mormones llega al valle Salt Lake para establecer su nuevo hogar.
The U.S. wins the Mexican War. Mexico gives Utah to the United States.	**1848**	E.U.A. gana la guerra méxico-americana y México le cede Utah.
Brigham Young becomes the first governor of the Utah Territory.	**1851**	Bringham Young es el primer gobernador del Territorio de Utah.
Utah becomes the forty-fifth state in the Union.	**1896**	Utah se convierte en el estado cuarenta y cinco de la Unión.
The state capitol is completed.	**1915**	Se completa el capitolio del estado.
Uranium is discovered near Moab.	**1952**	Se descubre uranio cerca de Moab.
The New Orleans Jazz basketball team moves to Salt Lake City and becomes the Utah Jazz.	**1979**	El equipo de baloncesto de los New Orleans Jazz se traslada a Salt Lake City y se transforma en los Utah Jazz.
The Winter Olympics take place in Salt Lake City.	**2002**	Las Olimpíadas de invierno tienen lugar en Salt Lake City.

Utah Events

January
Sundance Film Festival in Park City

April
St. Georges Arts Festival in St. Georges

June
Utah Arts Festival in Salt Lake City
Strawberry Days Festival in Pleasant Grove

July
Pioneer Days in Ogden
Mormon Miracle Pageant in Manti

August
Park City Arts Festival en Park City

September
Utah State Fair in Salt Lake City

December
Handel's Messiah in the Mormon Tabernacle in Salt Lake City

Eventos en Utah

Enero
Festival de cine Sundance, en Park City

Abril
Festival de las artes de St. Georges

Junio
Festival de las artes de Utah, en Salt Lake City
Festival de los días de la fresa, en Pleasant Grove

Julio
Días de los pioneros, en Ogden.
Procesión del milagro mormón, en Manti

Agosto
Festival de las artes de Park City

Septiembre
Feria del estado de Utah, en Salt Lake City

Diciembre
El Mesías de Handel, en el Tabernáculo Mormón, en Salt Lake City

Utah Facts/Datos sobre Utah

<u>Population</u> 2.2 million		<u>Población</u> 2.2 millones
<u>Capital</u> Salt Lake City		<u>Capital</u> Salt Lake City
<u>State Motto</u> Industry		<u>Lema del estado</u> Industria
<u>State Flower</u> Sego lilly		<u>Flor del estado</u> Lirio mariposa
<u>State Bird</u> California gull		<u>Ave del estado</u> Gaviota de California
<u>State Nickname</u> The Beehive State		<u>Mote del estado</u> Estado Colmena
<u>State Tree</u> Blue spruce		<u>Árbol del estado</u> Abeto azul
<u>State Song</u> "Utah, We Love Thee"		<u>Canción del estado</u> "Nuestra querida Utah"

Famous Utahans/Utaheños famosos

Reed Smoot
(1862–1941)
Politician
Político

Butch Cassidy
(1866–1908?)
Outlaw
Bandido

Virginia Sorensen
(1912–1991)
Writer
Escritora

Loretta Young
(1913–2000)
Actress
Actriz

James Woods
(1951–)
Actor
Actor

Steve Young
(1960–)
Football player
Jugador de fútbol americano

Words to Know/Palabras que debes saber

beehive
colmena

border
frontera

flatland
llanura

warrior
guerrero

Here are more books to read about Utah:
Otros libros que puedes leer sobre Utah:

In English/En inglés:

Utah
America the Beautiful Second Series
by Deborah Kent
Children's Press, 2000

Uniquely Utah
by Bianca Dumas, D. J. Ross
Heinemann, 2003

Words in English: 330

Palabras en español: 335

Index

A
Arches National Park, 10

B
border, 6

F
flatlands, 22

G
Great Basin, 8
Great Salt Lake, 8

H
Hispanics, 16

M
Mormon(s), 14

R
Rocky Mountain region, 6

S
Salt Lake valley, 14
seal, 4
Sundance Film Festival, 18

Índice

E
escudo, 4

F
Festival de cine Sundance, 18

G
Gran Cuenca, 8

H
hispanos, 16

L
Lago Great Salt, 8
llanuras, 22

M
Montañas Rocosas, región de las, 6

Mormón(es), 14

P
Parque Nacional Los Arcos, 10

V
Valle Salt Lake, 14